*For Isabella, Dante, Sofia, & Lisa...*
*my inspiration...my everything*

*Special thanks to Joy & Troy*
*(not just because your names rhyme)*

*And a super-duper special thanks to Lynn!*

THIS TAG NOT TO BE REMOVED
EXCEPT BY THE CONSUMER

ALL NEW MATERIAL CONSISTING OF
49% IMAGINATION
48% INSPIRATION
3% PERSPIRATION

REG. NO. HECK WHO KNOWS!

VIKING
Published by Penguin Group
Penguin Young Readers Group, 345 Hudson Street, New York,
New York 10014, U.S.A.

1 3 5 7 9 10 8 6 4 2

First published in 2005 by Viking,
a division of Penguin Young Readers Group

Honk-Honk-Ashoo & Swello-Bow-Wow ®
are registered trademarks of Ralph Cosentino

Manufactured in China

Copyright © Ralph Cosentino, 2005 • All rights reserved

The text is set in Vag Rounded, which has been
described as the most marvelous font ever.

LIBRARY OF CONGRESS
CATALOGING-IN-PUBLICATION DATA
Cosentino, Ralph.
The story of Honk-Honk-Ashoo &
Swello-Bow-Wow /
by Ralph Cosentino.
p. cm.
Summary: Honk-Honk-Ashoo
adopts a stray dog, making both
of them very happy.
ISBN 0-670-05997-8 (hardcover)
[1. Dogs—Fiction.] I. Title: The
story of Honk-Honk-Ashoo and
Swello-Bow-Wow. II. Title.
PZ7.C818555t 2005
[E]—dc22
2004005180

100% GUARANTEED COMFORT!

# The Story of
# Honk-Honk-Ashoo & Swella-Bow-Wow®

written & illustrated by

Ralph Cosentino

VIKING

There once was a pillow head

who snored his name:

Honk-Honk-Ashoo.

When the sun rose,

his night light would turn off

and his alarm would ring.

He then went outside

to do his exercises.

Exercise is very good for you.

Honk-Honk-Ashoo

always read the funnies while

having his breakfast.

Then he would

do his chores, with the help

of his wagon, Squeak.

When Honk-Honk-Ashoo

was finished, it was time to play.

One morning,

Honk-Honk-Ashoo's alarm

did not wake him, but some barking

at his front door did.

As he opened the door,

a scared little dog ran in.

A dogcatcher

was chasing the little dog.

"Is that your dog?" he yelled.

"No," said Honk-Honk-Ashoo.

The dogcatcher drove to the pound. Honk-Honk-Ashoo thought the little dog looked sad. He felt sad, too.

Honk-Honk-Ashoo

decided that neither of them

should be sad.

He adopted the little dog

and took her home.

The little dog was a little stinky,

so Honk-Honk-Ashoo gave her a bath.

For the rest of the morning,

they did everything together.

That afternoon, they went to the park

and met Honk-Honk-Ashoo's friend Soda.

He gave them a drink and said,

"This little dog is marvelous!"

"Marvelous" was a word

Honk-Honk-Ashoo did not know,

so he got help from his

friend Smarty Pants.

Honk-Honk-Ashoo said

to the little dog, "You *are* marvelous!

That means you are really swell.

Let's call you Swella-Bow-Wow!"

That night, Honk-Honk-Ashoo

and Swella-Bow-Wow went to bed

nice and early, together.